Monkey Ono

J. C. Phillipps

VIKING
An Imprint of Penguin Group (USA) Inc.

For Pat, who once had a stuffed monkey

VIKING
Published by the Penguin Group
Penguin Young Readers Group, 345 Hudson Street, New York, New York 10014, U.S.A.
Penguin Group (Canada), 90 Eglinton Avenue East, Suite 700, Toronto, Ontario,
Canada M4P 2Y3 (a division of Pearson Penguin Canada Inc.)
Penguin Books Ltd, 80 Strand, London WC2R 0RL, England
Penguin Ireland, 25 St Stephen's Green, Dublin 2, Ireland (a division of Penguin Books Ltd)
Penguin Group (Australia), 250 Camberwell Road, Camberwell, Victoria 3124,
Australia (a division of Pearson Australia Group Pty Ltd)
Penguin Books India Pvt Ltd, 11 Community Centre, Panchsheel Park, New Delhi – 110 017, India
Penguin Group (NZ), 67 Apollo Drive, Rosedale, Auckland 0632,
New Zealand (a division of Pearson New Zealand Ltd.)
Penguin Books (South Africa) (Pty) Ltd, 24 Sturdee Avenue, Rosebank, Johannesburg 2196, South Africa

Penguin Books Ltd, Registered Offices: 80 Strand, London WC2R 0RL, England

First published in the United States of America by Viking, a division of Penguin Young Readers Group, 2013

10 9 8 7 6 5 4 3 2 1

Copyright © Julie Phillipps, 2013
All rights reserved

LIBRARY OF CONGRESS CATALOGING-IN-PUBLICATION DATA
Phillipps, J. C. (Julie C.)
Monkey Ono / by J.C. Phillipps.
p. cm.
Summary: Left behind when his family goes to the beach, Monkey Ono enlists the help of Java the cat and Telly the dog
in a series of ill-conceived plans to join in on Beach Day.
ISBN 978-0-670-78505-6 (hardcover)
[1. Monkeys—Fiction. 2. Cats—Fiction. 3. Dogs—Fiction. 4. Humorous stories.] I. Title.
PZ7.P53725Mon 2013   [E]—dc23   2012016777

Manufactured in China   Set in Archer   Book design by Kate Renner

The art for this book was rendered mostly in cut paper collage, along with a little watercolor painting, crayon sketching, and some sewing.

ALWAYS LEARNING   **PEARSON**

Monkey Ono loved beach day and . . .

. . . making plans.
"It's called Operation: Beach Day!"
he said to Java the cat.
Monkey Ono went through the steps.

Monkey Ono heard the door shut
and the car drive away.

Oh noooo!

He ripped off his goggles.

He clobbered the floor.

Then . . .

BANANZA!

"I call it Operation: Telly Express,"
Monkey Ono said to Java and Telly.

"BOOM!
Beach Day!"

Telly seemed into it . . .

. . . until he buried Monkey Ono in the backyard.

Oh noooo!

"Operation: Swirlie!" Monkey Ono declared.

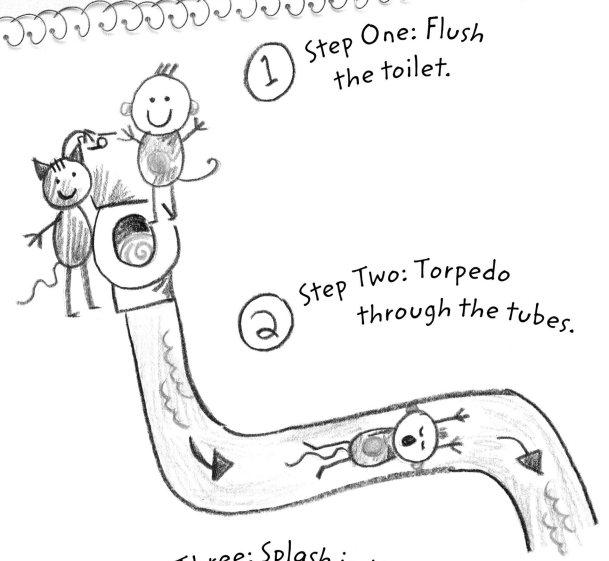

1 Step One: Flush the toilet.

2 Step Two: Torpedo through the tubes.

3 Step Three: Splash in the waves.

"**BOOM!**
Beach Day!"

Monkey Ono snapped on his goggles.
Everything went swimmingly until . . .

Splash... gurgle... GUSH!

Oh noooo!

Monkey Ono grabbed his crayon.
"Operation: Slingshot!"

Step One: Pull the hammock back.

Step Two: Release the hammock.

Step Three: Fly to the beach.

"BOOM!
Beach Day!"

Monkey Ono got into launch position.
He was certain his plan would go off
with flying colors.

Monkey Ono soared past the trees,
over the bushes, and . . .

. . . into the neighbor's yard.

Oh noooo!

"I give up!" said Monkey Ono.
"I'll never get to build a sand castle!"

"I'll never get to soak my feet!"

"I'll never get to watch fishies!"

Monkey Ono flopped on the floor.
"I'll never get my Beach Day!"
Then . . .

BANANZA!

All afternoon Telly dug holes in the sand,
Java napped in the flowerpot . . .

. . . and Monkey Ono made sand castles,
soaked his feet, and watched fishies.
Oh yeah!